THE SPOILER

ASHOK JAHAGIRDAR

Made with ♥ on the Notion Press Platform
www.notionpress.com

Contents

Prologue

"Life is never simply black or white—nor are people purely good or irredeemably bad. In Taoism, the yin, symbolized by white, represents virtue, while the yang, embodied in black, signifies chaos. Yet the paradox lies in their interdependence: alone, they are incomplete. Only when united do they form the whole - a harmony of opposites, where light defines shadow, and goodness gives meaning to evil."

CHAPTER ONE

Defying Dimensions

There once lived a tiny little man and his equally tiny little wife in a modest apartment. Their son, however, defied the "tiny" theme entirely. Tall, handsome, and dedicated to his studies, he was in the final year of his accountancy course. His romance, if it existed, won't feature here - he was far too serious for such distractions. Like his father, he had a gift for numbers.

The father, known to his colleagues as **"The Spoiler,"** worked as an accountant for a large firm. His nickname might seem peculiar now, but trust me, it will make sense as the story unfolds.

==

Five years ago, when the firm's owner was merely toying with the idea of starting the business, he wasn't convinced it would succeed. A friend of his recommended the tiny little man. Sceptical but desperate, the owner approached **"The Spoiler"** for his advice.

"The Spoiler" didn't rely on calculators. With a sharp mind and an uncanny ability to crunch numbers in his head, he confidently declared that the firm would turn a significant profit within two years, regardless of the economic climate. His conviction was so unshakable that the owner prepared the papers the very next day. The bank approved the loan, and the firm was launched with little fanfare.

This was 5 years back. Today the firm has far exceeded the prediction made by **"The Spoiler"**. It occupied 2 floors and has a employee count of 100. The owner keeps on gushing his gratitude to "The Spoiler" always responds with a weak smile, shrugs his shoulders and returns to his work.

CHAPTER TWO

How They Met (And How Numbers Led to Love)

The first time he saw her, it was in the university library—a place he treated like a second home. She was sitting at his usual table.

This was unacceptable.

==

He prided himself on routine. Every Monday, Wednesday, and Friday, he claimed the corner desk by the window at precisely 3:15 PM. It was optimal: natural light, minimal foot traffic, and a clear line of sight to the emergency exit (he had calculated the probability of a fire at 0.0037%). But today, a stranger had invaded his territory.

He hovered awkwardly, debating whether to ask her to leave. Then she looked up.

"You're blocking my light," she said, voice dry.

He blinked. "That's statistically impossible. The angle of the sun at this hour means - "

"- that you're still standing there," she finished, raising an eyebrow.

He sat down. Defeated.

==

She was studying law. She had no patience for nonsense, which, unfortunately, included his entire personality.

"You can't quantify everything," he told him once, when he tried to calculate the exact probability of her agreeing to coffee.

"I can try," he muttered.

She laughed—sharp, unexpected. "Fine. But if you're wrong, you owe me lunch."

(He was wrong. He didn't mind.)

==

They never had a formal proposal. It just... happened.

One evening, over takeout and tax forms, he slid a spreadsheet across the table.

"What's this?" she asked.

"Cost-benefit analysis of marriage," he said. "Tax advantages, shared living expenses, emotional ROI - all favourable."

She stared. "That's the least romantic thing I've ever heard."

"I know," he admitted. "But the numbers don't lie."

She sighed, then reached into her bag and pulled out a legal pad. "Fine. Here's my counteroffer: joint custody of the coffee machine, veto power on ugly furniture, and you never, never use the word 'ROI' in bed."

He considered it. "Deal. "

==

They signed the paper with a pen he borrowed from behind his ear.

CHAPTER THREE

The Wedding (Efficient and Effective)

The ceremony was small. His father - "The Spoiler"—spent the entire reception muttering about *"unnecessary variables."* His mother just smiled and said, "Took you long enough."

Her family, meanwhile, was delighted. "Finally," her brother said, "someone who can stop her from arguing with the microwave."

==

At the altar, when the priest asked for vows, he handed her another spreadsheet.

"Lifetime projections," he whispered.

She rolled her eyes—then kissed him before he could explain the inflation adjustments.

(The numbers, for once, were irrelevant.)

==

The young couple, recently married, had settled into their daily routines. The father-in-law, a man with a penchant for sharing unsolicited opinions, had once given his daughter-in-law a skewed idea of what life with his son might be like. But she didn't mind - she knew the truth.

CHAPTER FOUR

The Discrepancy

One evening, the husband informed his wife he'd be late returning from work. A few discrepancies in the accounts had caught the chief auditor's attention, and he insisted on a thorough review. The husband, known for his precision and integrity, agreed to stay back.

He was, after all, a man who could find a needle in a haystack. He also knew his father would retire early after dinner, as usual.

==

During the meal, the father-in-law turned to his daughter-in-law with a smug smile and said, "Did you know my son was terrible at studies? If not for my intervention, he wouldn't have cleared his exams."

What he didn't know was that his daughter-in-law had been her husband's classmate in college. She knew, as did everyone on campus, that her husband had been a consistent topper - renowned not only for his academic brilliance but also for his unshakable honesty and integrity.

Feigning surprise, she replied, "Oh, is that so? He failed every exam?"

Unaware of her sarcasm, the father-in-law nodded, oblivious to the truth. But the conversation left her with a bitter taste. She contemplated sharing her thoughts with her husband that night but decided against it.

==

The next morning, she continued her usual routine, sending breakfast to her father-in-law. Despite the lingering resentment, she upheld her grace and composure, determined to maintain peace in the household.

That morning, as the breakfast tray clinked gently in her hands, she paused at the threshold of her father-in-law's room. A polite knock, a neutral smile, and the tray was placed before him without a word. He didn't notice the silence. He rarely did.

She returned to the kitchen, her fingers still tense from the effort it took to remain composed. Her husband hadn't returned until well past midnight. She had left the lamp on and his dinner warm, but he had gone straight to their room and fallen asleep, too exhausted to speak. He hadn't seen the flicker in her eyes or the weight she had quietly carried through the night.

==

By evening, things were back to their familiar rhythm. Her husband, freshly showered and rested, joined her for tea. He looked at her across the rim of his cup and asked gently, "Everything okay at home yesterday?"

She hesitated. There was a moment—one heavy with possibility—when she could have told him everything. About his father's arrogance, the distorted stories, the quiet insult hidden in paternal pride. But instead, she smiled and said, "Just the usual. Your father told me about your glorious academic failures."

He laughed. "He's still going on about that?" He shook his head.

"You'd think he raised a genius single-handedly."

"You are a genius," she said, setting her cup down. "But apparently, he gave you that too."

There was humour in her voice, but it didn't quite reach her eyes.

Later that night, as they folded laundry together, he spoke again. "You don't have to take it all in silence, you know. If he oversteps—just say it. I'll handle it."

She looked at him, searching his face. "It's not about handling," she said quietly. "It's about choosing what to carry and what to let pass. Some things aren't worth a fight."

==

He nodded slowly, sensing there was more beneath her words. He reached for her hand and gave it a gentle squeeze.

That weekend, her husband received a letter of commendation from the audit board—his meticulous work had saved the firm from a potential loss. The news was shared at the breakfast table. The father-in-law beamed with pride.

"My son always had a sharp mind," he declared loudly. "Got it from me."

She met her husband's gaze. He gave her the smallest of smiles. In that silent exchange, they shared the one thing the old man would never understand: truth didn't need defence. It simply endured.

The commendation letter remained on the mantle for a week, framed and polished, its edges catching the morning light like a silent rebuttal to the past. Yet in the quiet corners of the home, tension lingered like a perfume that refused to fade. Politeness reigned, but warmth had begun to wear thin.

==

It was a Sunday afternoon, the kind that invited rest—but rest had become a luxury neither of them truly felt. She was in the kitchen, folding the last of the dish towels, when he came to her with a stillness in his voice that made her stop mid-fold.

"I've been thinking," he said. "We need our own space."

She didn't look surprised. In truth, she had been thinking the same, but hadn't dared say it. Not because she feared her husband's reaction—he had always been fair—but because a part of her still clung to the hope that perhaps things would smooth over. That his father's barbed comments would dull, that patience would be enough.

But patience, she had come to realize, wasn't a cure—it was just a pause.

She looked up at him, the towel now a forgotten thing in her lap. "Are you sure?"

He nodded. "Yes. I know my father. It's just that he seems to get joy in someone else's sorrow. And I can't ask you to keep bending for someone who doesn't see how much strength that takes. You've been gracious long enough."

==

For a moment, neither of them spoke. Outside, a koel called from the gulmohar tree. Inside, something settled between them—a sense of quiet relief.

CHAPTER FIVE

Edge of the City, Edge of Tomorrow

By the next weekend, they had found a modest two-bedroom flat on the edge of the city. It wasn't large, but it was theirs. The air smelled of new paint and old dreams. She unpacked the kitchen first—her hands moving swiftly, confidently—as if the cabinets themselves were a promise of fresh beginnings.

==

On their first night there, they ate dinner on the floor, the furniture still in transit. He brought out two glasses and a bottle of juice. She laughed. "Is this our housewarming party?"

"No speeches," he said, raising his glass, "just peace."

She clinked her glass against his. "Peace."

Later, as they lay on a mattress surrounded by unopened boxes, he turned to her and said, "You didn't say much when I brought up moving out."

She traced her finger along the crease in the bedsheet. "Because I've already said so much to myself. Every day, in silence."

He nodded. "You'll never have to do that again."

And in that dimly lit room, filled with cardboard and exhaustion and the scent of something new, she believed him.

CHAPTER SIX

Stitches in Time

It began with a phone call neither of them expected.

The father-in-law had been hospitalized—nothing life-threatening, just a minor fall at the office that required a few stitches and overnight observation. The call came from a junior colleague, nervous and apologetic.

"I didn't know who else to call... he didn't want anyone, but I thought you should know."

The son listened in silence, then thanked him. He hung up and stood still for a long moment.

She looked up from the book she was reading. "You're going," she said. It wasn't a question.

He nodded. "I have to."

She closed the book gently. "Then I'm coming too."

==

The hospital was dimly lit and quiet by the time they arrived. The nurses directed them to his room without fanfare. He was awake, sitting upright, a bandage on his forehead and the same scowl on his face that he'd worn at every family function for the past year.

The moment he saw them, his jaw clenched.

"Did someone call you?" he snapped. "I didn't ask anyone to call."

"We came because we wanted to," the son replied evenly.

She stood beside him, calm, composed. Not warm - just respectful. The silence hung heavy between them until the nurse walked in to check his vitals. The conversation paused, but the air thickened.

When the nurse left, the old man looked at his son and said, "You left this house. Your mother's house. You abandoned your responsibility."

It wasn't new—but this time, the words landed differently.

"I didn't abandon anything," the son said, voice steady. "I built a life. I took care of you even when I was being belittled under your roof."

"I raised you -"

"You controlled me," he cut in, firm but not angry. "And for years, I let you. I let you rewrite my success as yours. I let you treat my wife like a servant in her own home. I kept thinking if I worked harder, you'd change. That maybe you'd finally see me for who I really am. But I've realized something - your approval is not a prize I need to win."

The father-in-law's eyes widened - not in fear, but in something close to disbelief. He had always expected silent resistance, never this clarity, never this calm rebellion.

She stepped forward now, her voice low but clear. "We didn't leave because we were weak. We left because we were strong enough to protect what you refused to respect."

"And now what?" the old man snapped. "You come here like saviours? Like you're better than me?"

"No," the son said. "We came because we're not like you."

==

The room fell into a heavy, echoing silence.

The "**The Spoiler**" looked away first.

They didn't stay long after that. A polite conversation with the doctor, a quick thank-you to the nurse, and they walked out into the night air - cool, sharp, clean.

In the parking lot, the son exhaled as though he hadn't breathed in years.

She reached for his hand. "You okay?"

He nodded. "I think... I finally said what I needed to say."

"No yelling," she said with a small smile. "I'm proud of you."

He looked at her, then back at the hospital window glowing faintly above them.

"Maybe he'll never change."

"Maybe," she said. "But we did."

==

They got into the car, drove home in silence, and stepped back into their apartment - still cluttered with books, laughter, burnt toast memories, and light.

It wasn't perfect.

But it was theirs.

CHAPTER SEVEN

Empty Rooms, Hollow Days

A few months passed, and the silence of the house began to wear not just on the furniture but on the man who sat alone within it.

The father-in-law, once surrounded by the buzz of his son's presence and the silent competence of his daughter-in-law, now found his days long and uneventful. The television droned endlessly, the same news cycles and serials. Even the neighbours had grown quieter—polite, but distant. He was no longer the patriarch of a bustling home; he was just an aging man with opinions and no one to correct.

One morning, without much ceremony, he dusted off his old briefcase, ironed his shirts with a precision only he cared about, and returned to the office.

His colleagues were surprised. He had officially retired two years earlier, but he walked into the building like he had never left. The head of the department, after a bit of stumbling and awkward courtesy, offered him a consulting role - part-time, advisory.

He accepted it with a grunt and a nod, as though it were his idea all along.

In the weeks that followed, the office felt his presence like a returning winter: crisp, cold, and sharp around the edges. The Spoiler barked at juniors for formatting errors, dismissed ideas he didn't like with a snort, and handed out unsolicited lectures about "how things were done in his time."

"The Spoiler" never mentioned his son's commendation or promotion. In fact, when someone brought it up in the break room, he waved it off.

"He got lucky," he muttered. "Would've failed his final year if not for me pushing him every night."

==

No one dared challenge him - not out of respect, but because his words carried that peculiar bitterness that comes from wounded pride. His authority was tolerated, not welcomed. But he didn't care. In his mind, he was back where he belonged: in control, above reproach.

One afternoon, as he walked past a conference room, he caught sight of his son's name on a document projected on the screen.

"Joint audit strategy – recommended by – his son's name stared at him."

==

"The Spoiler" paused. Listened. The younger team was discussing how the new framework his son had designed was being used across branches.

He scoffed, just loud enough to be heard. "All theory. Let's see how it survives real-world pressure."

==

Later that evening, back home, he sat at his dining table with a reheated meal and the memory of a different dinner—one with the quiet strength of a daughter-in-law who listened more than she spoke, and a son who used to smile even through his father's corrections.

He shook the thought off and turned up the television. But the voices couldn't quite drown the growing echo in the rooms.

==

Meanwhile, across town, his son had returned home to the scent of cardamom and curry leaves. His wife was humming an old song in the kitchen, barefoot and radiant with flour on her cheek.

"How was work?" she asked, handing him a glass of water.

He smiled and leaned against the wall. "Busy. Fulfilling."

She caught something in his voice - a shadow, maybe. "Is he doing okay?"

He shrugged. "Back at work. Barking orders. Acting like he never left."

She nodded and said nothing more. She had learned long ago that not all wounds want bandages. Some just need space.

That night, as they stood on the balcony, looking out at the stars, she reached for his hand.

"You did the right thing," she said.

"I know," he whispered.

But neither of them smiled.

Not yet.

Three Years Later

Over the following months, the father-in-law made his presence known—not in their home, but in the shadows of their professional and social circles. He never visited, never called, but found ways to remind them that he had not approved, not forgotten, and certainly not forgiven.

Word trickled in through mutual acquaintances, colleagues, and distant relatives. **"The Spoiler"** had become something of a one-man campaign, casually undermining his son's achievements at family gatherings, suggesting that his daughter-in-law had "seized control" of the house, and implying that modern couples had no spine, no sense of duty.

But the couple had moved beyond needing his permission.

At first, the comments stung. Her husband would return home after overhearing something at work—a snide remark slipped in by an old associate loyal to his father—and she would see the flicker of hurt behind his eyes. She knew it well. He didn't say much, but he didn't need to.

She would take his hand, hand him tea, draw him into the comfort of their shared silence. And in those small gestures, he found the fortitude to keep going.

==

Their new home became a refuge. With no one watching, they began to craft a life that reflected their values—quiet, simple, honest. He started reading again, something he hadn't done since college. She enrolled in an evening course on art therapy and surprised herself with how much joy it brought her.

They celebrated small victories: a dinner that turned out perfectly, a weekend with no work emails, a walk that ended with unexpected rain and shared laughter. The absence of criticism, the absence of walking on eggshells - it made room for something richer.

They learned to talk—not just about errands or work, but about fears and memories, about what hurt and what healed.

One evening, after a particularly cutting remark from his father had been relayed to him by a relative, he sat in the balcony, unusually quiet.

She joined him, two mugs of warm milk in hand. He took his, held it for a moment, then said, "You know, for a long time, I thought if I worked hard enough, he'd finally respect me."

She didn't rush to respond. Instead, she placed her hand on his knee and said softly, "You don't need his respect to be who you are. He didn't build you. You did."

==

That night, something shifted. Not loudly, not with some grand epiphany - but like a stone finally sinking to the bottom of a calm pond.

They stopped listening to the echoes of the old house. When someone tried to pass along his father's comments, her husband would politely change the subject. When a relative tried to stir drama, she would smile and redirect the conversation toward what book they were reading.

They created a shield not of anger, but of clarity. They knew the truth of who they were. And that was enough.

==

In time, their home grew warmer—not with applause or approval from the world, but with purpose. Friends began to visit. A small herb garden flourished on the balcony. They hosted their first Diwali alone and didn't miss the grandeur. What they had was light of another kind.

And while the "**The Spoiler**" remained the same - bitter, proud, determined to diminish - his shadow began to shrink, not because he changed, but because they had outgrown it.

CHAPTER NINE

Coffee, Turmeric, and Moving On

What was once hurt now became history. And history, they learned, doesn't have to be carried forever.

The apartment still smelled of filter coffee and turmeric. Morning sunlight spilled across the floor in gentle ribbons, touching the framed photographs on the wall—moments frozen in time: their first anniversary, a vacation by the sea, and a candid shot of them both laughing, her head thrown back, his eyes soft.

In the kitchen, a small hand reached up to tug at her kurta.

"Mumma, dosa ready?"

She smiled and bent down to kiss her daughter's forehead. "Almost, sweetheart. Go tell Papa to get the plates."

The little girl scampered off. Seconds later, her husband appeared in the doorway, mock-saluting. "Reporting for breakfast duty."

They laughed, as they always did—easily, quietly, with the intimacy of people who had weathered storms together.

As they sat down to eat, a soft ding echoed from her phone. She glanced at it, expecting a work message or school update. But the sender made her pause.

"Appa : Hope your little one is well. There's a box coming your way. Some of her grandmother's books. She would've wanted her to have them.

It waas a terse message from her father-in-law, "**The Spoiler**".

==

She stared at it, the words blinking gently like a heartbeat. No apology. No invitation. Just a gesture. Subtle. Stark. Maybe even sincere.

She handed the phone to his son. He read the message once, then again. A long breath escaped him.

"Well," he said quietly, "that's new."

She reached for his hand under the table, fingers interlacing with his.

"What do we do?" he asked.

"We do what we've always done," she replied. "We receive what's given. And we protect what's ours."

==

He nodded slowly. "We've built something good, haven't we?"

She looked around the sunlit room. Their daughter now playing with building blocks in the living room, the smell of dosa lingering, a half-read book on the armrest of the couch.

"Yes," she said. "Not perfect. But deeply, honestly ours."

==

And as the city stirred beyond their windows, full of noise and lives and stories not unlike theirs, the couple sat at their breakfast table - hands entwined, hearts steady - knowing that the past could haunt, but it could no longer hurt.